margaret Tempest.

FUZZYPEG'S
BROTHER

The Little Grey Rabbit Library

FUZZYPEG'S BROTHER

BY ALISON UTTLEY

PICTURES AFTER MARGARET TEMPEST

Collins

First published in Great Britain by
William Collins Sons & Co Ltd in 1971
This edition published by
HarperCollins Publishers Ltd in 1994
Text copyright © The Alison Uttley
Literary Property Trust 1994
Illustrations copyright © HarperCollins
Publishers Ltd/The Estate of Margaret Tempest 1994

Illustrations after the style of Margaret Tempest
by Mary Cooper

Alison Uttley's original story
has been abridged for this book.

A CIP catalogue record for this title
is available from the British Library.

ISBN 0 00 193407-4

Produced by HarperCollins Hong Kong

This book is set in Goudy

Collins

An Imprint of HarperCollins*Publishers*

FOREWORD

Of course you must understand that Grey Rabbit's home had no electric light or gas, and even the candles were made from pith of rushes dipped in wax from the wild bees' nests, which Squirrel found. Water there was in plenty, but it did not come from a tap. It flowed from a spring outside, which rose up from the ground and went to a brook. Grey Rabbit cooked on a fire, but it was a wood fire, there was no coal in that part of the country. Tea did not come from India, but from a little herb known very well to country people, who once dried it and used it in their cottage homes. Bread was baked from wheat ears, ground fine, and Hare and Grey Rabbit gleaned in the cornfields to get the wheat.

The doormats were plaited rushes, like country-made mats, and cushions were stuffed with wool gathered from the hedges where sheep pushed through the thorns. As for the looking-glass, Grey Rabbit found the glass, dropped from a lady's handbag, and Mole made a frame for it. Usually the animals gazed at themselves in the still pools as so many country children have done. The country ways of Grey Rabbit were the country ways known to the author.

Little Fuzzypeg, the Hedgehog, had a baby brother, and he was very proud of this new little companion. The baby was grey and his tiny prickles were soft as feathers instead of being sharp as needles.

"They'll grow hard and sharp like yours when he is older," said Mrs Hedgehog, as she rocked her baby in his cradle of rushes.

"Shall we call him 'Prickles'?" asked Fuzzypeg.

"No, we are going to call him 'Little Urchin'," replied Mrs Hedgehog. "'Urchin' is our family name going right back to the time when the Romans lived here."

She stroked her baby softly to make his spines rattle, and Fuzzypeg whispered, "Little Urchin. That's a nice name."

Little Urchin slept, and woke for milk, and slept again, and he kept on growing.

In a few weeks he could toddle after his mother, and soon he began to play with Fuzzypeg under the trees.

One day he came running very fast into the house.

"There's a something in the trees," cried Urchin. "It went whoof! whoof! and it frightened me."

"What is it like?" asked Mrs Hedgehog, stroking the little prickles.

"I don't know. I can hear it, not see it," said Urchin. "It howls and shakes the trees."

Mrs Hedgehog stood listening. Then she laughed. "It is only Mr Wind, Little Urchin. He won't hurt you."

"It makes me feel cold when he blows at me," said Urchin.

"The wind is a friend of animals," said Mrs Hedgehog. "He ruffles the grass so that man can't see us. He carries the scent of man to us and warns us. He dries us when we are wet."

In the garden a line of clothes hung from a thin rope stretched from a rose-bush to a tall foxglove. There was a pair of tiny pyjamas, and a jersey, a leafy handkerchief and a scarf.

"The wind is blowing them to dry them," she said. "It huffs and it puffs to blow out all the wet drops."

The wind gave a tug and away flew the pyjamas, dancing, running, leaping in the air, and after them ran Urchin. He caught the truant pair.

"The wind is having a game with you," said Mrs Hedgehog, laughing.

Fuzzypeg made a little windmill out of a stick with four large nut leaves pushed into a crack. Then he ran across the grass, and the wind turned the sails of the windmill as he ran with it held out.

Mr Hedgehog gathered some long rushes from the damp corner of the common, and Mrs Hedgehog wove them in an oval shape to make a hammock.

"What is this for?" asked Fuzzypeg, watching her fingers weave the green rushes backward and forward.

"I am plaiting a hammock. You will see," promised his mother.

Next morning they found the hammock hanging from the branches of a tree.

"It is Little Urchin's day-bed, so that he can swing safely in the wind's arms," said Mrs Hedgehog.

She lifted the hedgehog inside. Then he swung to and fro, as the wind swayed the hammock. This was a fine game and Fuzzypeg also climbed in.

Old Hedgehog brought Grey Rabbit and Hare to see the baby hedgehog.

Grey Rabbit was enchanted by the tiny fellow. She brought a rattle made of poppy seeds and a little red smock.

Hare brought a wooden horse which he had made out of a small branch of a crooked little tree.

"It's for you to ride, Urchin," he said and he sat on it himself and danced up and down the field.

"I shall take my brother to school," said Fuzzypeg to Grey Rabbit.

"Is he old enough?" asked Grey Rabbit, peeping at the tiny hedgehog. "He is only a baby."

"I'm not a baby!" said Urchin indignantly. "I'm a big hedgehog, Grey Rabbit." He danced and rolled in a ball of prickles like his father.

"I'll go to school too," said Hare.

The next day they set off, Hare and Fuzzypeg and Little Urchin. The schoolroom was a patch of short grass, hidden among the gorse bushes where nobody could see what was happening. It was safe from foxes and hawks and dogs with its prickly walls.

The grass was covered with little daisies and clover and blue milkwort and tiny yellow pansies.

Old Jonathan, the schoolmaster, stood waiting, and he welcomed the baby hedgehog. The little fellow sat on the grass, among a lot of small animals – a few rabbits and squirrels, a young hare, a cousin of Hare's and some field-mice who could not keep still.

Old Jonathan shook his stick at them. "Silence all, and welcome to Little Urchin."

So everyone settled down quietly, although the mice swished their tails and whispered.

"Counting lesson first as usual," said Old Jonathan.

They all stood in a circle and sang their old counting song with actions:

"One, two, buckle my shoe." They stooped down and fastened the grassy shoe-laces on their feet.

"Three, four, knock at the door," they sang, and the animals tapped on the brass knocker of the school door, and tapped on the ground too.

"Five, six, pick up sticks," they sang, and all, with Little Urchin racing after them, gathered up the scraps of sticks which lay by the bushes.

They laid them in straight tidy lines.

"Seven, eight, lay them straight," they chanted in their tiny squeaky voices, like birds.

Urchin suddenly tripped and rolled over. Old Jonathan frowned and picked him up and tidied him.

"Nine, ten, a good fat hen," sang the company and then they all flapped their arms and cried, "Cluck! Cluck! Cluck!" like the Speckledy Hen.

Jonathan stooped over the sticks and took a thick glass from his pocket. He held it in the rays of the sun that shone down on them. The sun sent a band of light through the glass on to the sticks, a tiny scrap of smoke arose, and a point of fire shone. The sticks were alight.

"Oh Sir, how did you do that?" the rabbits asked.

"A burning-glass," said the schoolmaster. They all clapped their fists.

"Time for the next lesson," said Jonathan. "It is reading. Everybody can read our books, which hang on the trees."

He gave a leafy twig book to each animal, and every book had a complete tiny story written on the green pages.

Jonathan gave a book to Urchin, but he put it in his mouth and ate it up, so his story was lost.

A little rabbit read the first story, and they all sat quietly listening as she held the leaves and read the pages.

"There was a little house,
And in it lived a mouse.
She ate a piece of cheese,
And flew into the trees,
And then began to sneeze."

They clapped their paws as she sat down.
Then another rabbit read aloud:

"I saw a busy bee,
He drank a mug of tea.
He ate a scrap of honey,
And found it very funny.
He gave a taste to me."

Hare then read a story from his book:

"There was a prickly Hedgehog,
As prickly as a pin.
He had a little cushion,
To keep his needles in."

Fuzzypeg clapped his paws. "That's me," said he,
and he read a story.

"There was a little worm,
And it could never turn
To left or to right,
Although it tried all night,
And so it went
  STRAIGHT ON."

"That was a nice tale," said Urchin. "I do wish I
had not eaten my story-book."

"Playtime," said Old Jonathan. "You read your books well. I am proud of you."

They danced and leapt; they climbed trees and dropped to the ground; they chased and rolled down the grassy banks. They played Kiss-in-the-Ring with a shy little rabbit in the middle and Fuzzypeg kissed her.

Hare jumped over four animals standing in a row, and Urchin rolled in a ball.

Jonathan spoke: "Come along, my pupils, and have some new milk." A cow had come to look at them and her face peeped over the bushes. Jonathan milked her and filled their mugs with creamy frothy milk.

It was delicious and they all had sips, and then threw their tiny mugs over the hedge.

"Guessing Game," said Jonathan. They sat in a circle, and he asked questions.

"What flowers are yellow?" he asked.

"Primrose, cowslip, buttercup, oxlip, dandelion," they shouted.

"Which flower is red?" asked Jonathan.

Hare said, "Red campion."

Fuzzypeg said, "A red rose, but wild roses are pink."

"Which flower is white?" asked Jonathan, and they answered:

"Daisy, daisy," and there was such a noise the cow took fright and went away.

"What else?" asked Jonathan.

"White campion," said Hare, proud of his knowledge.

"White clover," said Fuzzypeg.

"Snowdrops," said a rabbit.

Little Urchin knew nothing of these names, but he ran and picked some flowers when the lesson ended.

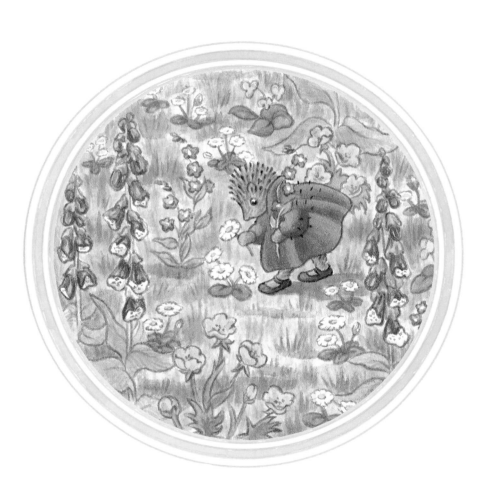

They were packing their school bags when there was a knock on the brass knocker. Jonathan opened the door carefully lest there should be a fox. There was nobody, but a string was fastened to the knocker, and on the ground lay a bright blue ball. There was a letter fastened to the ball.

Jonathan untied it and read aloud slowly.

"A present to Urchin from the south-west wind."

"Urchin!" he called. "It is for you. It's a balloon, filled with wind to play with." They all crowded round, but Jonathan took Urchin by the paw.

"Very careful," said he. "You must keep your prickles away or it will burst."

"Oh! Oh! Oh!" cried Urchin.

The south-west wind was blowing. He puffed at the balloon, and Urchin was lifted off his feet.

Up in the air he went and everyone tried to catch his dangling feet.

"Oh thank you, Mister Wind!" called Urchin as he was swept across the grass, with his toes on the buttercups.

"He's flying!" shouted the animals.

"Hold fast, Urchin!" Fuzzypeg called.

"Yes," squeaked the breathless Urchin. "It's lovely, flying."

Then the wind dropped him softly so that his feet touched the ground.

Hare asked Urchin to let him try. He held the string and ran fast, but the balloon only bobbed on the grass, refusing to rise up.

"Go away," muttered the wind, blowing at his legs, and he had to give the string back to Urchin.

"Time to go home," said Old Jonathan. "Take care of the blue ball, Urchin," he added, and little Urchin set off home, half flying, half walking. Across the grass went the mob, with Urchin leading.

Mr Hedgehog was as excited as anybody when he saw the beautiful balloon.

"We'll keep it outside," said he. "It will be safer, away from our prickles," and he tied it to a low branch of a tree where it was hidden by the leaves.

"It is a present from the wind himself," said Mrs Hedgehog excitedly when she read the note. "I always said he is a friend to us."

So every day a blue balloon could be seen bobbing near the green, flying across the fields, and down into the valley. Some children tried to catch it but they never got near enough. The wind took care of the little hedgehog dangling from a string, swinging and waving his paws as he touched a flower with his toes.

Summer was over and autumn came, bringing wild winds and making the clouds scurry over the sky. Up very high the Snow King was preparing for winter. He got his flocks of snow ready to send to the earth, and he told Jack Frost to sharpen his icicles ready to stab the water and freeze it. The little balloon shivered with cold. Fuzzypeg and Urchin slept for hours and the balloon was lonely.

"Winter is coming, and we must keep the balloon safe," said Mrs Hedgehog. "We'll keep it in the woodshed while we have our winter sleep. It is warm and safe and the balloon can rest until spring comes."

Fuzzypeg and Urchin nodded, as they watched their father tie the balloon to a log of wood, where it tossed in a tiny wind coming through the keyhole.

"Go to sleep, little balloon," said Urchin, and the balloon sighed and slept.

So winter passed and nobody went to school. Doors were shut and sleepy creatures slept.

The spring came, and the south wind blew, and the violets and primroses pushed up their buds and opened their eyes. The little balloon gave a tug at its string.

Grey Rabbit looked out at the sunshine.

"Winter has gone," said she. "I will go out and have tea with Mrs Hedgehog, and see how Urchin has slept." She put two new laid eggs from the Speckledy Hen in her basket, and set off. She picked a bunch of primroses, and a yellow butterfly settled on them and went with her.

"How is the balloon?" she asked, as she sipped the fragrant herb tea and smiled at everybody.

"Come and see it," invited Mrs Hedgehog. Little Urchin clapped his paws, Fuzzypeg unlocked the door of the shed, and they ran inside.

There hung the blue balloon, tugging at the string, bobbing with excitement. Round its head was a garland of cowslips and primroses.

"Where have those flowers come from?" asked Mrs Hedgehog astonished.

Nobody knew. The door had been locked, but Spring must have crept through the keyhole.

"It is a present from Spring to hedgehogs," explained Grey Rabbit. "I think you could go out with your balloon now," said she, smiling at Fuzzypeg.

"The gorse will soon be in flower and then you can go to school." They untied the string and took the eager little balloon out to the common.

Off went Urchin, dangling his tiny feet above the flowers of spring, with Fuzzypeg shouting after him, and Grey Rabbit waving her handkerchief.

Nobody was as happy as Fuzzypeg's brother, as he floated over the gorse bushes pricked with yellow. He looked down at Old Jonathan, the schoolmaster, who lay asleep in a corner with his head on a pillow of primroses.

"No school today," murmured Jonathan sleepily. Then he opened an eye and saw the balloon with the Urchin.

"Hello, young fellow," he cried. "A happy Easter to my clever scholar."